OCEAN TOMB

by ANTHONY MASTERS

Illustrated by Tim Sell

W
FRANKLIN WATTS
NEW YORK • LONDON • SYDNEY

First published in 1997 by
Franklin Watts
96 Leonard Street
London
EC2A 4RH

Franklin Watts Australia
14 Mars Road
Lane Cove
NSW 2066

Series editor: Helen Lanz
Art Director: Robert Walster
Designer: Sally Boothroyd
Special Needs Consultant: Pat Bullen,
Head Teacher of Moderate Learning
Difficulties, Bitham School
Reading Consultant: Frances James

A CIP catalogue record for
this book is available from
the British Library.

ISBN: 0 7496 2797 2
Dewey Classification: 363.12

10 9 8 7 6 5 4 3 2 1

Printed in Great Britain

Contents

DANGER ZONE

FACT FILE

LOCATION

2,250 km off the south-west coast of Australia in the Southern Ocean

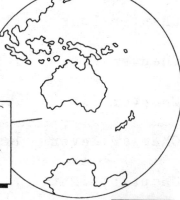

DANGER

Capsized, or overturned, yacht *Global Exide Challenger*. Lone yachtsman Tony Bullimore surviving in upturned boat.

PERSONNEL

Tony Bullimore

HAZARDS

- ! Freezing water
- ! Limited drinking water and food supply
- ! Two-thirds of boat filled with water -
  air supply therefore reduced
- ! Possibility of life-raft floating free and
  causing rescue search to be called off
- ! Little finger ripped off at joint
- ! Severe frostbite

The Global Exide Challenger

CHAPTER
ONE

Testing weather

Winds suddenly reached the amazing speeds of 50 to 55 knots in the Southern Ocean.

Fifty-seven-year-old Tony Bullimore was competing in the Vendée Globe single-handed round-the-world yacht race in his yacht, *Global Exide Challenger*.

He had planned to take about 120 days to complete the 35,420 kilometres.

• Towering waves

Stirred up by the wind, the waves started to build. Soon they were enormous - towering above him.

Bullimore had seen the storm coming. He had taken down the sails and his yacht was running under bare poles. He tied himself to the helm and hoped to ride out the weather.

● Automatic pilot

As evening came, Bullimore was exhausted and put his yacht on automatic pilot so it would steer itself.

He then went below and sat down on the step by the cabin entrance. From there, he could keep an eye on the deck.

Bullimore made a cup of tea and ate some chocolate biscuits. He was feeling good, pleased that his yacht was dealing so well with such terrible weather.

Bullimore was 1,450 km from Antarctica and 2,250 km off the Australian coast.

Then disaster struck.

Chapter Two

Capsized!

Suddenly, the yacht lurched to one side.

As Bullimore stood up, he heard a crack and the boat did a somersault.

The hull, or bottom of the boat, was now the top. Bullimore found himself standing on the ceiling of the cabin.

Bullimore realised that his five-metre keel, the long steel board which was keeping the yacht upright in the water, had snapped off.

There was no chance the boat could turn the right way up now.

● Cool and experienced

But Bullimore was a highly experienced
yachtsman. He had always been resourceful.
He didn't panic and sat down to think
coolly about what he could do.

It was night. He was grateful that the lights
were still working inside the boat.

Chapter Three

A place of safety

At dawn, the yacht's boom worked loose.
It started tapping against the window,
now at the bottom of the boat.

Suddenly, the window collapsed.

The sea rushed in.

• A water-filled cabin

The freezing water came in with such force that it hit the top of the hull. Sea water filled the cabin, knocking out the lights. The water stopped coming in when the hull was two-thirds full.

The waves rocked the yacht to and fro. This meant that the sea only entered the boat through the broken window.

The sea swirled around fiercely, sucking objects out and ripping things off the walls.

Bullimore climbed into a watertight survival suit. The water was getting deeper.

● A narrow space

Searching desperately for a place of safety, he noticed the storage shelf which was half-a-metre wide. This was originally just above floor level. Now, with the yacht overturned, the shelf was up by the ceiling.

Bullimore managed to wedge himself into the narrow space, by lying on his stomach and holding on with one hand.

He then rigged up some cargo netting into a hammock so that he wouldn't roll off into the water.

Now he could concentrate on surviving.

Chapter Four

Plans for survival

Bullimore's situation was terrifying. He knew his best chance of survival was to stay with his yacht and wait to be rescued.

He also knew it would take at least two days for any rescue services to reach him.

The air in the hull was limited by the presence of so much water. The supply of oxygen was in danger of running out.

● More problems

Part of Bullimore's little finger had been torn off when he had caught it in a door just after the yacht had capsized.

His feet were bitterly cold inside his rubber boots. He kept banging them against the side of the boat to try and warm them up.

His only supplies were a tin of baked beans, some chocolate and a limited amount of bottled drinking water.

● A test of survival

Another problem was his life-raft. If this floated free from the wreck, rescuers might assume that he was dead and call off their search.

To avoid this, Bullimore had to make sure the life-raft stayed tied to the boat.

He spent four out of every twelve hours diving under the water and swimming to the life-raft to make sure it was secure.

This was a great test of survival. But Bullimore knew he had to keep going.

Chapter Five

Alive!

Bullimore lay crammed on the shelf and in his hammock. The freezing water swilled around below him.

He ordered his thoughts. He was very strict about what he allowed himself to think.

To begin with, he concentrated on forming possible escape plans.

One idea was to make the upside-down hull seaworthy and float to Antarctica. Another was to use the life-raft.

● An escape plan

Now, Bullimore was desperate enough to try
and escape in the raft.

Diving down, with a knife between his
teeth, Bullimore swam to the raft to see
if he could ease the craft out of the hull.

But there was no way he could push it out
into the open sea.

● Food supplies

The worst part of the waiting was that he was hungry and knew exactly where his main food supplies were.

There were tins of corned beef, boxes of milk, soft drinks and biscuits.

But Bullimore knew if he opened any of the airtight hatches where the food was kept, then the yacht would start to sink.

● A distress signal

. All competitors in the race in which Bullimore was taking part had to carry an EPIRB - an emergency radio beacon.

These can be switched off. They can also be set to send an alert signal or a distress signal via satellite to the Vendée race headquarters.

Some of these beacons will start automatically when in water. They often transmit for many weeks.

● Still alive

Bullimore had three emergency beacons. At the start, two of them had been on deck. One of them was later found by the Australian Navy. It was still transmitting 32 kilometres away from the yacht.

The third beacon was inside the hull.
Bullimore decided to turn the signal on
and off himself.

He hoped that anyone who heard it would
realise that he must be alive.

Chapter Six

A strong will

Despite all his courage, Bullimore was beginning to realise that his options were running out.

He was facing death.

● The need to sleep

The cold was beginning to spread into his body. He could feel it creeping into his lungs.

If the upper part of Bullimore's body got too cold, it wouldn't warm up again.

His heart would begin to beat more slowly, his mind would become confused.

The urgent need to sleep, whatever the conditions, would overcome him.

● Discipline and control

Bullimore still controlled his thoughts. He knew if he allowed himself to think that he was going to die, this would lower his morale and weaken his chance of survival.

● The will to survive

Instead, he remembered the happiness of his marriage and his family and friends.

Then, he began to pray for the strength to last just one more day.

Bullimore disciplined himself to survive.

Chapter Seven

Rescued

Bullimore was in his hammock again, when he heard the sound of a propeller plane. He listened carefully.

Could it be that he might be rescued?

He didn't dare swim outside the upturned hull. If it was a false alarm he knew that he wouldn't have the strength to get back again.

● A voice

Bullimore heard banging on the hull. The banging had a pattern to it. Then he heard a voice.

Immediately, Bullimore jumped down into the water and started banging back. He yelled out that he was alive - and was coming out fast.

● Gripped by terror

Then a dreadful terror gripped him.

Suppose his rescuers hadn't heard him shouting? Suppose they went away and left him to die?

Bullimore ducked down into the freezing water. He moved as quickly as he could through the upturned boat.

He let himself through the hatch. He swam as deep as he could to avoid getting tangled in the rigging.

When he reached the surface
he could hardly believe his eyes.

● The best moment

Alerted by Bullimore's manual signal,
the Australian Royal Navy Frigate HMAS
Adelaide was standing by.

A plane was flying overhead and a couple of
men were on the top of the upturned boat.

Everybody on board the *Adelaide* was cheering.

Bullimore knew this was the best moment of his life.

● A happy embrace!

Bullimore was pulled up into a rubber speedboat. One of his rescuers was a diver named Chief Petty Officer Pete Whicker.

Bullimore told him that if he hadn't got a beard he would have kissed him.

Whicker told him to go ahead anyway and they embraced!

Chapter Eight

A hero's welcome

Bullimore had no bottled water left and could not have lasted another twenty-four hours.

The oxygen supply in the hull of the upturned yacht would also have run out.

• Surgery

The HMAS *Adelaide* took him to Perth in Australia. There, he had surgery to save his frostbitten finger and had his feet treated.

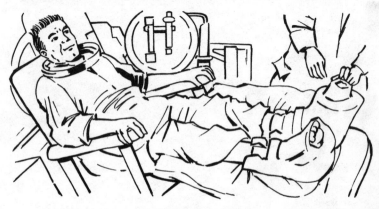

● Beer and a sandwich!

Thousands of people had crowded on to the quayside at Fremantle where the *Adelaide* docked. It was a hero's welcome.

Bullimore was asked whether he needed counselling after his extreme experiences at sea. Bullimore replied he would rather have a beer and a sandwich!

● A strong personality

Tony Bullimore's strong personality and his resourcefulness had made sure he survived.

In many ways, Bullimore's entire life had been an exercise in survival. He had had to work hard in his younger days to get by.

The capsize in the freezing waters of the Southern Ocean was only one more test.

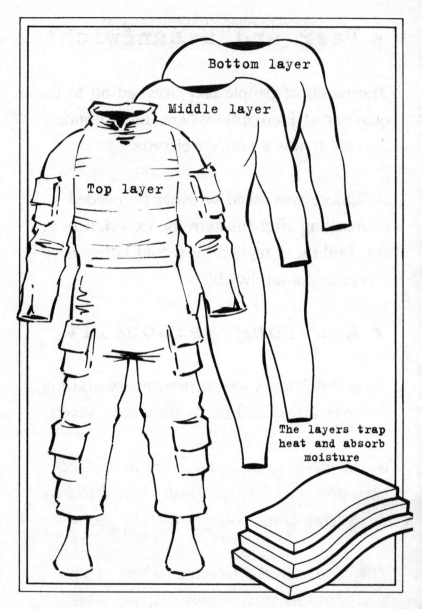

Bottom layer

Middle layer

Top layer

The layers trap
heat and absorb
moisture

The British Dry Suit

FURTHER FACTS

- Bullimore's survival suit saved his life during the long hours of waiting for rescue. It is called a British dry suit. It helped to protect him from frostbite and hypothermia (a condition when the body temperature gets very low).

- The dry suit is made to provide three hours' survival time in water. It has three protective layers.

- The bottom layer absorbs sweat from the body. This helps to keep the person dry and warm.

- The middle layer traps air. This builds another layer of warmth.

- The top layer keeps out the wind and water. It protects the person from bad weather conditions.

- The Vendée Globe yacht race is a round-the-world race for single-handed sailors. It is one of the world's most dangerous courses.

- The yachts must be single-hulled boats. They can only be between 15 metres and 18 metres long.

- The course crosses the Southern Ocean. Yachts can go faster here because there is more wind. But conditions can be treacherous. Boats are a long way from help if they need assistance.

- Among the dangers are icebergs, the temperature of the sea (about 6°C), the strength of the wind (which can reach 70 knots) and the height of the waves (which can reach six metres).

GLOSSARY

Bare poles: this is a phrase used in sailing to mean when the boat is travelling with the sails down.

Boom: the long pole on a boat that holds the bottom of the sail.

Capsized: when a boat has turned over.

Counselling: when a trained person helps someone to come to terms with a difficult situation in his or her life.

EPIRB: Emergency Position Indicating Radio Beacon.

Frostbite: when body-tissue is damaged from being exposed to extreme cold.

Hammock: cloth or netting hung up by the ends to form a bed.

Helm: the steering equipment of a ship.

Hull: The body of a ship.

Hypothermia: When the body temperature sinks so low it could cause death.

Rigging: the mast, sails and tackle (or ropes) of a ship.

IMPORTANT DATES

1997

January 5th	Day 1: Winds reach speeds of 50-55 knots, waves build to great heights and *Global Exide Challenger* capsizes.
January 6th	Day 2: Boom works loose and breaks reinforced window. Freezing water comes in, filling hull two-thirds full.
January 7th	Day 3: Bullimore now in survival suit and in improvised hammock. He changes signal on emergency beacon.
January 8th	Day 4: Cold begins to take hold of Bullimore's body. He is in danger from hypothermia and frostbite.
January 9th	Day 5: Bullimore hears banging on hull and dives out. He swims to the surface to be rescued by HMAS *Adelaide*.